THE JUNIOR GREAT BOOKS

DISCUSSION PROGRAM

✝

The Junior Great Books

SERIES ONE · VOLUME TWO

5
DUVOISIN
The Three Sneezes and Other Swiss Tales
SELECTIONS

6
SAWYER
Picture Tales from Spain
SELECTIONS

7
HATCH
13 Danish Tales
SELECTIONS

8
PERRAULT
Fairy Tales

ROGER DUVOISIN

The Three Sneezes
and Other Swiss Tales
SELECTIONS

NUMBER **5**
SERIES ONE

THE GREAT BOOKS FOUNDATION *Chicago*

published and distributed by

THE GREAT BOOKS FOUNDATION
a nonprofit corporation
307 North Michigan Avenue, Chicago, Illinois 60601

THE THREE SNEEZES
AND OTHER SWISS TALES

JEAN-MARIE THE FARMER climbed up a tree to cut some wood for his stove. His donkey, standing below, closed his eyes and went to sleep.

Just then a stranger on horseback happened to pass by. "Heh, there," cried the stranger, "have you ever sawed wood before?"

"Why, if all the wood I have sawed in my life was gathered together it would make a fine forest," Jean-Marie shouted back.

"One wouldn't think so," said the stranger.

"Why not?" demanded Jean-Marie.

"Because when you have sawed through that branch on which you are sitting, both you and the branch will fall to the ground."

"Be off with you, stranger," said Jean-Marie. "I can see that you know nothing about sawing wood."

So the stranger went off, and Jean-Marie went on sawing. Presently there was a terrible crash, and both he and the branch fell to the ground.

Jean-Marie picked himself up, and when he had rubbed all his bruises and found that his back was not broken, he bethought himself of the stranger's words. "Surely that was a wonderful man," he thought, "for he told me that the branch and I would fall to the ground, and so we did. He must know the future. I will go after him, and ask him a thing or two."

So Jean-Marie got on his donkey, and away they went after the stranger. Presently they came to a turn in the road, and there was the stranger, ambling along on his horse as though nothing had happened.

"Ho, there!" cried Jean-Marie.

"What is it?" said the stranger, stopping his horse.

"I see that you can read the future, so I want to ask you a thing or two."

"What makes you think I can read the future?"

"You said that when I had sawed through the branch, both of us would fall to the ground, and so we did."

"Oh," said the stranger, smiling, "I see. Well, ask me your questions, but I warn you I can only answer one of them."

"Very well," said Jean-Marie, "just answer me this. When am I going to die?"

"That's easy," said the stranger. "You will die when your donkey has sneezed three times." And with that he rode away.

"My donkey never sneezes," thought Jean-Marie, "so I shall live a long time." And he started for home feeling very happy.

Now donkeys are very stubborn, and they always do just the very thing they should not. When they should walk, they will not budge, and when they should keep still they are always walking away. So it was not very long before the donkey opened his mouth and . . .

"Aatshoum!" he sneezed, loud and long.

Jean-Marie was aghast. All his happiness was changed to terror. He jumped down and pressed both hands against the donkey's nose to stop the next sneeze (for everybody knows one always sneezes more than once). When the danger seemed past, he resumed his trip, but now he did not dare to ride. Instead, he walked beside the donkey so as to prevent any more sneezes.

Presently they came to a freshly plowed field, and there Jean-Marie paused to admire the rich brown earth. What a fine crop of wheat would grow there next summer. Forgetting all about the sneezes, he bent down to feel it with his hands, and . . .

"Aaatshoum!" sneezed the donkey for the second time.

Jean-Marie snatched his hat and put it over the donkey's nose and held it tight.

"Two sneezes already! Two horrible sneezes!" he lamented. "I am only one single sneeze from death, one miserable donkey sneeze. Surely I am the most unhappy man alive. I am sure that stranger must have been the devil. He not only told the future, he is making my donkey sneeze. He bewitched my donkey!"

But he was holding the hat too tightly over the donkey's nose, and the donkey, finding he could not breathe, reared up and kicked Jean-Marie very severely.

"Some other remedy must be found," said Jean-Marie. "For if my donkey sneezes again I am a dead man."

Then he had an idea. He picked up two round stones and placed them in the donkey's nostrils, like corks in a bottle. "There, just let him try to sneeze that out," he thought. But he had reckoned without the contrariness of donkeys.

"Aaaatshoum!"

The stones flew out like bullets from a gun. They hit Jean-Marie in the face.

"Ah! Ah!" said Jean-Marie. "I am dead. Very, very dead."

And he lay down in the road, for it is not right for a dead man to stand up.

FOR LACK OF A THREAD

THERE WAS ONCE a mouse and a coal who went for a walk.

Across their path they found a stream. The mouse thought nothing of it. She jumped in, and swam to the other side. But the coal dared not go into the water.

"There," cried the mouse, throwing over a straw. "Take this and cross the stream on it."

Alas! The coal in midstream set fire to the straw and was drowned, saying, "Sssssssst!"

At this the mouse began to laugh, and she laughed so hard and so long that she burst.

So she went to the shoemaker, to borrow a needle to sew herself up again.

"I will sew you up," said the shoemaker, "if you will go to the sow and get some thread, for I have none."

The mouse went to the sow and said, "Give me some thread for the shoemaker who will sew me up."

"I will gladly give you some thread," said the

sow, "if you will go to the miller and get me some bran."

The mouse went to the miller and asked, "Will you give me some bran for the sow, who will give me some thread for the shoemaker, who will sew me up?"

"I will gladly give you some bran," said the miller, "if you will go to the field and get me some wheat."

The mouse went to the field and asked, "Will you give me some wheat for the miller who will give me some bran for the sow who will give me some thread for the shoemaker who will sew me up?"

"I will gladly give you some wheat," said the field, "if you will go to the ox and get me some manure."

The mouse went to the ox and asked, "Will you give me some manure for the field who will give me some wheat for the miller who will give me some bran for the sow who will give me some thread for the shoemaker who will sew me up?"

"I will gladly give you some manure," said the ox, "if you will go to the meadow and get me some grass."

The mouse went to the meadow and asked, "Will you give me some grass for the ox who will give me some manure for the field who will give me some wheat for the miller who will give me some bran for the sow who will give me some thread for the shoemaker who will sew me up?"

"I will gladly give you some grass," said the meadow, "if you will go to the river and get me some water."

The mouse went to the river and asked, "Will you give me some water for the meadow who will give me some grass for the ox who will give me some manure for the field who will give me some wheat for the miller who will give me some bran for the sow who will give me some thread for the shoemaker who will sew me up?"

The river said nothing, and asked for nothing, and gave the mouse a bucketful.

The mouse took the water to the meadow who gave her an armful of grass.

She took the grass to the ox who gave her a basketful of manure.

She took the manure to the field who gave her a sheaf of wheat.

She took the wheat to the miller who gave her a bag of bran.

She took the bran to the sow who gave her a spool of the finest thread, and with this the mouse rushed to the shoemaker. But the shoemaker could not sew up her belly, for now she was dead.

LONG AGO, as everyone knows, the earth was full of fairies, and there were as many fairies in Switzerland as anywhere else. There were bad ones and good ones, but those that lived around the village of Clèbes in Valais were exceptionally good. They did all manner of charitable acts. They helped the poor; they cured the sick; they guided the herdsmen as the cows were led to the high alpine pastures; they cleaned the chalets. In short they were the very best of fairies.

They were seldom seen by the villagers, but one day a young man named François had the good fortune to meet one as he was going up to the *alpage,* the high pasture. She was picking blue gentians to make a nosegay. She was so lovely that François fell in love with her on sight. Instantly he asked her to marry him.

The fairy said (for to tell the truth she was not in love) that she could not marry him; that fairies are forbidden to marry mortal men. But François pleaded so insistently and seemed so sincerely in love, and was, after all, such a fine-looking herds-

8

man, that at length she yielded. Placing her hand upon his shoulder, she said, "François, I can become your wife on one condition: you must never be angry with me, and you must never, never say, 'You are a bad fairy.' "

François gave his solemn promise.

So they were married in the church. The traditional cow was killed for the feast, and the village fiddlers, perched on two empty wine-casks, played for the dance. It was a gay wedding, and promised a happy life.

And indeed they were to live many happy years together. They never quarrelled. They had three pretty children. When François came home at night after a hard day's work in the field or on the mountain, he would find his children so well taken care of, the wood walls so white, the supper so good, and his wife so cheerful, that he felt himself a lucky man, as indeed he was.

But on a certain summer day François was called to the Alp of Maïens to tend an ailing cow. The sky was darkening when he left, and the air was warm and heavy. Fearing a storm François did not stay long at his alp-chalet, but giving his instructions to the *pâtre,* he hurried homeward.

Now fairies have knowledge of the future, and possess the secret of avoiding misfortune. In the valley François' fairy-wife knew that a terrible hail storm was coming. Quickly, with the aid of other Alp fairies, her friends and kinsfolk, she harvested her wheat. It was still green and flowering, but nevertheless they brought it in and stored it in the barn with a branch of alder-tree between each sheaf.

Hardly had this been done when the storm broke. It was the worst storm the mountaineers had seen for many years. Hailstones as big as apples fell upon the valley and devastated the fields. The desolate peasants were ruined. Hunger would be their lot during the long winter that lay ahead.

François had arrived home just as the storm began. When he learned what his wife had done in his absence he flew into a violent rage, and brutally reproached her.

"Who ever harvested green wheat?" he screamed. "The hail might have spared some of our wheat. Now all of it is lost. It will rot, every bit of it. Ah! You are a bad fairy!"

As the words left his lips there was a sinister noise like a snake whistling and thrashing its tail, and his wife vanished before his eyes. But this did not abate his anger. Leaving his children in tears, he stamped out to the barn to examine the wheat.

How wonderful! From floor to rafters the barn was crammed with the most magnificent wheat, golden and ripe. The huge heads were bursting, and fat hard grains were falling to the floor! François had expected to find a mass of green festering wheat. How unjust he had been to his wife!

But François was a stupidly stubborn man. "Just the same she shouldn't have done it," he said to himself.

He went slowly back to the house. All his children were sitting at table, and the dinner was served.

"Who served the dinner?" asked François.

"Mother."

"Where did she go?"

"We don't know. She didn't say. She only said that you should apologize for your hard words. It is not too late if you do."

"Apologize? No, no. Never!" said the vain and stubborn François.

He dined alone and slept little that night. He was unhappy. Yet he would not say the words that would bring back his wife and his happiness.

The next morning he found his children washed, dressed, and combed. Their breakfast was served, but his was not. The fairy again was warning him to apologize, but François remained stubbornly silent.

Several days later he drove to the miller to have his wheat ground. How the miller's eyes popped when he saw the bags full of beautiful grain.

"How can you have such fine wheat, François, and so much of it, when the whole harvest has been destroyed?" he asked. "You are the only man in the valley to have any wheat at all."

François told him what had happened.

"Now I know that you are a fool," declared the miller; "twice a fool, since you refuse to apologize. You don't deserve to have such a wonderful wife. Go home and beg her pardon."

François made up his mind then and there. He would apologize. The decision made him happy, and loading the heavy bags of flour into his cart, he drove quickly home.

Everything was upset in his house. The cat slept in the bread chest; the milk pails were black with flies; the sink was a mountain of dirty dishes. Only the children were still washed and neatly dressed.

"When your mother comes," François told them, "tell her I will apologize now."

The next morning he was wakened from sleep by a gentle tap on his shoulder. It was his little girl.

"Mother has come," she said. "She says she will remain if you will kiss the first thing you find behind the kitchen door."

François jumped out of bed and ran to the kitchen, filled with joy. There was nothing behind the door. He thought it must be a joke. Then he heard again that whistling noise which had sounded when his wife vanished, and looking down he beheld an ugly snake. It coiled and uncoiled at his feet. Then it climbed up around him until its head hung level to his face.

It swayed right and left waiting for the kiss. But François' repulsion was too strong. He grabbed the snake and flung it on the floor, where it vanished, and instead his wife stood before him.

"If your love is not stronger than your repulsion," she said, "you do not deserve my pardon. I now abandon you, your fortune, and your children. You are a proud, vain, and stubborn man," and she vanished forever.

François knew that all was lost, but though his grief was great, it was now too late. In the years that followed he became poorer and poorer, and in the end he and his children were obliged to go from farm to farm begging for work or a little food that they might keep alive. And the fairy wife was never seen again.

JACOB found life most arduous. In his father's chalet at the edge of the forest which darkens the foot of the Gemmi, he did nothing but complain from morning till night.

"Why isn't every day Sunday?" he lamented when he had to get up at dawn to milk the cows, or carry a load of fresh grass to the rabbits.

"If only I could lie down and dream," he sighed as he went down to the communal oven to fetch the brown bread in his pack-basket.

"I should have been born rich, like some people. I shouldn't have to toil and toil, like an ox," he grumbled.

"Nothing good ever happens to a lazy boy like you," said his old mother. "You will become poorer and poorer."

"Unless I get rich quickly."

"Yes. But how?"

"I know an easy way," laughed the hunchback from Leuk.

14

"Do you really?" asked Jacob.

"Yes. I know an enchanted rock on the Torrenthorn, with a rich treasure hidden inside. If you follow the rules, the rock will open."

"Tell me the rules then. Quick, tell me. I want to go."

"At midnight you must lie on a cowhide near the rock. A mysterious clock will slowly strike the twelve strokes of midnight. At the first stroke the rock will open. Then hurry, hurry, hurry, gather as much of the treasure as you can before the twelfth stroke, for the rock closes then. Many have lingered behind and been crushed. It is said that no one has yet come out of the rock alive."

"Oh, I will know when to go. Have no fear."

That very night Jacob set out with a bag folded in his pocket. He bought an old cowhide at Leuk, and started for the Torrenthorn. With the cowhide tied on his back so that his hands were free, he began to climb the steep Albinen ladders. It is much more exhausting to climb a mountain than to milk a cow, or skim the milk, but Jacob did not stop to think of that. He climbed and climbed, with the slow steady steps of the mountaineer, until he came to the rock which the hunchback had described. Here he spread the cowhide on the rough grass, lay down, and waited impatiently. He had come up so fast that he had to wait a long time.

The first stroke of the mysterious clock was repeated by the echoes of the valleys. With a noise of rusty chains trailing on the ground, the rock split wide open. Jacob rushed in. He marveled at the round piles of silver standing side by side like piles of stones set along the side of a road. Quickly he filled his bag, listening to the clock which was slowly but steadily striking the midnight hour.

At the fifth stroke he had already filled his bag, and was grieved at not having brought a larger one. Then, seeing a door ahead, he ran through into a second room. What a sight! Here were piles of gold, even bigger than the piles of silver.

Bang . . . bang . . . boomed the clock.

"I have time," thought Jacob. He threw the silver on the ground, and hurriedly filled the bag with gold until it almost burst.

Bang . . . bang. . . . The mysterious clock continued to strike the hour.

"I have time," thought Jacob, lifting the bag on his shoulder. "Let's see what is behind this second door."

How wonderful! The floor of the third room was covered with diamonds up to Jacob's knees. He waded through them as one wades through a swamp.

Bang . . . bang . . . bang . . .

"Never mind," thought Jacob. "I still have time."

He emptied the bag of gold, and began to fill it with diamonds.

Bang! . . . The clock boomed, and stopped. The twelve strokes were over. Hardly had the echoes died, when the rock began to close, with the same din of rusty chains.

Terrified, Jacob ran back toward the entrance, slipping over the gold and silver he had thrown on the floor. He squeezed through the narrowing crack. On his shoulders he could feel the pressure of the closing rocks. He was out! But the rock caught his bag, and crushed the diamonds, like millstones grinding wheat to flour.

The fright and the excitement had been too much for Jacob. He fainted. When he came to, he was lying on the cowhide, with the sun, like a big round cheese, peering at him over the Torrenthorn. Jacob thought that he must have had a nightmare. The rock behind him was smooth and ordinary looking. It did not seem like a rock with a secret. But Jacob searched for his bag in vain. It was no longer folded in his pocket. It was inside the rock.

Sadly he returned to his home, where he lay ill with a high fever for some weeks. When he recovered, he was also cured of his desire to get rich quickly, and ever after he was a hard-working farmer.

RUTH SAWYER

Picture Tales from Spain
SELECTIONS

NUMBER **6**
SERIES ONE

THE GREAT BOOKS FOUNDATION   *Chicago*

published and distributed by

THE GREAT BOOKS FOUNDATION
a nonprofit corporation
307 North Michigan Avenue, Chicago, Illinois 60601

PICTURE TALES FROM SPAIN

THE SACK OF TRUTH

IT MAKES MANY YEARS in Spain since there was a king who had only one daughter. Since the Infanta was born she had been sickly. Years passed. As she grew older she grew no better; the royal doctors could find no cure for her malady.

"If the doctors of Spain are know-nothings, we will send for those of other countries," said the King.

That brought doctors from everywhere, and only one of them could mention a cure. He was a small Arabian doctor and he said: "Send for the finest pears in Spain. Enough of them will cure her."

So the King ordered pears—baskets of them. Whoever should bring in the best ones and cure the Infanta should have the wish of his heart granted. The King swore it by the good Santiago, patron saint of all Spain.

Many came bringing good pears and bad pears, yellow and green pears, juicy and withered pears; and the Infanta would eat none of them.

Outside a small village there lived a peasant with

1

three sons. Close to their hut grew a pear tree that every summer was covered with heart-shaped, fragrant pears, the color of gold.

One day the peasant said to the oldest son: "Take a basket, fill it with pears, take it to the King's palace and see can you not cure the Infanta."

The oldest set out with his basket, covered to keep the insects off. On the road he came up with a sad-faced woman carrying a little child. She stopped him and asked: "Boy, where are you going?"

"That isn't your business."

"What does your basket hold?"

"Horns!"

"Then let them be horns!"

Sure enough. When the oldest son reached the palace and uncovered his basket, it was filled with horns. So angry was the King that he ordered him thrown into the dungeon.

After a bit, when the oldest son did not return, the peasant said to the second son: "Something has happened to your brother. Go you, fill a basket with pears and try your luck."

The second son set out. On the road he came up with the sad-faced woman carrying the little child.

She stopped him and asked: "Boy, where are you going?"

"That isn't your business."

"What does your basket hold?"

"Stones."

"Then let them be stones!"

Sure enough. When the second son reached the palace and uncovered his basket, it was filled with stones. If the King had been angry before, now he was purple and bursting. He ordered the second son thrown into the dungeon with his brother.

After a bit, when neither son returned, the peasant caught the youngest, whose name was Pedro, filling a basket under the pear tree. He was sad, frightened. "What are you doing? You cannot go. How shall I run the farm with no sons? Why should you be thinking that the youngest will succeed where the oldest has failed?"

The youngest shook his head. No one had ever thought him very clever, only kind and willing and cheerful. "There is the old saying, you know," he said at last—" 'The fingers of one hand are never equal.' I may find luck where my brothers missed it."

So Pedro set out with his basket of pears. On the road he came up with the sad-faced woman carrying a little child. She stopped him and asked: "Boy, where are you going?"

"Mother, I am going to the King's palace."

"What does your basket hold?"

"Pears, to cure the Infanta of her long sickness."

And he thought to himself: "I must not be greedy with those pears. There is the old saying—'He who plays the fox for a day, pays for a year.' " So he uncovered the basket quickly, took out a pear and held it towards the child, saying: *"Nene,* would you like it? It is for you."

The woman took it for the child, smiling, and said: "Then let them be pears to cure! And for the one you have given away, ask what you will in return."

Pedro thought hard. "I would like a whistle which will call to me any animal I choose when I blow it."

"Here it is," said the woman, and she drew out of her kerchief a silver whistle strung on a cord so that Pedro could hang it around his neck.

When he arrived at the palace and uncovered his basket before the King, there were the pears, heart-shaped, fragrant, the color of gold. The King was overcome with joy when he saw them. "They are the best pears in the world!" he cried. "We will take them to the Infanta and see will she eat one."

The Infanta ate one—two—three. She would have eaten them all if the court doctor would have let her. Already there was a faint health showing in her cheeks.

"What do you want?" asked the King.

"My brothers."

The King had them released. Pedro was grateful. He thought of the old saying: 'Gratitude is better scattered than kept in one's pocket.' So he climbed the nearest mountain, blew on his whistle and called to him a wild hare. This he carried to the King. "Mark him, he is yours. Then free him. When I come back I will call him to you again. It shall be a sign between us of two men of honor."

But the King was astonished. "That is beyond your power to call back a wild hare. Nevertheless, if you do it, you shall marry the Infanta."

Over the world went Pedro with his silver whistle; calling to him creatures of all kinds, great and small, fierce and gentle. These he used in good service to others, and you can see how that might be.

At the end of a year he returned to Spain and the King's palace. But while he was still a long way off he blew for the hare and it came running to him, the King's mark still on him. The King saw them approaching from the balcony, the hare under Pedro's arm. He called for his prime minister. "There is that boy back again and with him the wild hare. You must bargain the creature away or I shall have to let him marry the Infanta."

Pedro sold the hare to the minister for a pound of gold. And when he had gone he whistled the hare back to him.

From his balcony the King watched. He saw what had happened. He was frantic—frantic. He called the under-minister. "Go bargain for that hare; and after you have paid for it, see that you don't lose it as the prime minister did. Hurry, hurry."

The under-minister had to pay two pounds of gold for the hare; and before he had reached the palace gates with it, Pedro had whistled it back again. "This is terrible—terrible!" said the King when he saw what had happened. This time he sent the Infanta, who returned saying that Pedro would only bargain with the King.

So the King went. Pedro drew him into the shadow of a plane tree. "You may have the hare for nothing, Your Majesty, if—you will kiss him."

The King was outraged. But what could he do? "Look carefully about. Is there anyone looking?" he asked.

"No one."

The King kissed the hare, just where Pedro's finger pointed. He followed the King back to the palace. Inside, in the Hall of Justice, before the entire court, Pedro asked: "You will keep your promise, yes? I marry the Infanta?"

But the King did not want that. Who ever heard of an Infanta of Spain marrying the son of a peasant? It was abominable. He must think of a way out. The prime minister thought of it and whispered in the King's ear: "Tell him he must take a sack, travel the world over and fill it with truth."

The King told Pedro what he must do first if he was to marry the Infanta.

"Good. Fetch me a sack."

The King sent for a large sack.

Pedro took it. He opened the mouth of it until it gaped wide. He said: "I have no need to travel to find truth enough to fill it. King, answer me: Is it not the truth that I brought a basket of the best pears to the palace?"

"It is."

"Truth, go into the sack," and he made a motion as if flinging it inside. "King, is it not the truth that those pears cured the Infanta?"

"It is."

"Truth, go into the sack. King, is it not true that

I gave the wild hare to you as a sign between us of two men of honor?"

"It is."

"Truth, go into the sack. King, is it not the truth that you put your mark upon that hare, freed it; and that I brought it back to you again?"

"It is."

"Truth, go into the sack. King, is it not the truth that in order to escape your promise and get the hare from me you kissed . . ."

"Stop!" said the King. "The sack is full of truth."

"And I marry the Infanta?"

"Agreed."

In a day they were married; in a year they had a son; in another year, a daughter. But it took a lifetime for them to get to the end of their happiness.

THE FLEA

ONCE THERE WAS and was not a King of Spain. He loved to laugh; he loved a good joke as well as any common fellow. Best of all he loved a riddle.

One day he was being dressed by his chamberlain. As the royal doublet was being slipped over the royal head, a flea jumped from the safe hiding-place of the stiff lace ruff. He landed directly upon the King.

Quicker than half a wink the King clapped his hand over the flea and began to laugh. *"Por Dios,* a flea! Who ever heard of a King of Spain having a flea? It is monstrous—it is delicious! We must not treat her lightly, this flea. You perceive, my Lord Chamberlain, that having jumped on the royal person, she has now become a royal flea. Consider what we shall do with her."

But the chamberlain was a man of little wit. He could clothe the King's body but he could not add one ribbon or one button to the King's imagination. "I have it!" said the King at last, exploding again into laughter. "We will pasture out this flea—in a great cage—large enough for a goat—an ox—an elephant. She shall be fed enormously. When she is of a proper size I will have her killed and her skin made into a tambourine. The Infanta, my daughter, shall dance to it. We will make a fine riddle out of it. Whichever suitor that comes courting her who can answer the riddle shall marry with her. *There* is a royal joke worthy of a King! Eh, my Lord Chamberlain? And we will call the flea Felipa."

In his secret heart the chamberlain thought the King quite mad; but all he answered was: "Very good, Your Majesty," and went out to see that proper pasturage was provided for Felipa.

At the end of a fortnight the flea was as large as a rat. At the end of a month she was as large as a cat who might have eaten that rat. At the end of a second month she was the size of a dog who might have chased that cat. At the end of three months she was the size of a calf.

The King ordered Felipa killed. The skin was stretched, dried, beaten until it was as soft, as fine, as silk. Then it was made into a tambourine, with brass clappers and ribbons—the finest tambourine in all of Spain.

The Infanta, whose name was Isabel, but who was called Belita for convenience, learned to dance with Felipa very prettily; and the King himself composed a rhyme to go with the riddle. Whenever a suitor came courting, the Infanta would dance and when she had finished, the King would recite:

"Belita—Felipa—they dance well together—
Belita—Felipa; now answer me whether
You know this Felipa—this *animalita*.
If you answer right, then you marry Belita."

Princes and dukes came from Spain and Portugal, France and Italy. They were not dull-witted like the chamberlain and they saw through the joke. The King was riddling about the tambourine. It was made from parchment and they knew perfectly well where parchment came from. So a prince would answer: "A goat, Your Majesty." And a duke would answer: "A sheep, Your Majesty"—each sure he was right. And the Infanta would run away laughing and the King would roar with delight and shout: "Wrong again!"

But after a while the King got tired of this sheep and goat business. He wanted the riddle guessed; he wanted the Infanta married. So he sent forth a command that the next suitor who failed to guess the riddle should be hung—and short work made of it, too.

That put a stop to the princes and dukes. But far up in the Castilian highlands a shepherd heard about it. He was young, but not very clever. He thought—it would be a fine thing for a shepherd to marry an Infanta, so he said to his younger brother: "Manuelito—you shall mind the sheep and goats; I will go to the King's palace."

But his mother said: "Son, you are a *tonto*. How should you guess a riddle when you cannot read or write, and those who can have failed? Stay at home and save yourself a hanging."

Having once made up his mind, nothing would stop him—not even fear. So his mother baked him a *tortilla* to carry with him, gave him her blessing and let him go.

He hadn't gone far when he was stopped by a little black ant. "Señor Pastor," she cried, "give me a ride to the King's court in your pocket."

"La Hormiguita, you cannot ride in my pocket. There is a *tortilla* there which I shall have for my breakfast. Your feet are dirty from walking, and you will tramp all over it."

"See, I will dust off my feet on the grass here and promise not to step once on the *tortilla*."

So the shepherd put the ant into his shepherd pouch and tramped on. Soon he encountered a black beetle who said: "Señor Pastor—give me a ride to the King's court in your pocket."

"El Escarabajo, you cannot ride in my pouch.

There is a *tortilla* there which I shall presently have for my breakfast—and who wants a black beetle tramping all over his breakfast!"

"I will fasten my claws into the side of your pouch and not go near the *tortilla*."

So the shepherd took up the beetle and carried him along. He hadn't gone far when he came up with a little gray mouse who cried: "Señor Pastor, give me a ride to the King's court in your pouch."

But the shepherd shook his head. "Ratonperez, you are too clumsy and I don't like the flavor of your breath. It will spoil my *tortilla* that I intend to have for my breakfast."

"Why not eat the *tortilla* now and then the breakfast will be over and done with," and Ratonperez said it so gently, so coaxingly, that the shepherd thought it was a splendid idea. He sat down and ate it. He gave a little crumb to La Hormiguita, a crumb to El Escarabajo and a big crumb to Ratonperez. Then he went on his road to the King's court carrying the three creatures with him in his pouch.

When he reached the King's palace he was frightened, frightened. He sat himself down under a cork tree to wait for his courage to grow.

"What are you waiting for?" called the ant, the beetle and Ratonperez all together.

"I go to answer a riddle. If I fail I shall be hanged. That isn't so pleasant. So I wait where I can enjoy being alive for a little moment longer."

"What is the riddle?"

"I have heard that it has to do with something called Felipa that dances, whoever she may be."

"Go on and we will help you. Hurry, hurry, it is hot in your pouch."

So the shepherd climbed the palace steps, asked for the King and said that he had come to answer the riddle.

The guard passed him on to the footman, saying, *"Pobrecito!"*

The footman passed him on to the lackey, saying, *"Pobrecito!"*

The lackey passed him on to the court chamberlain, saying, *"Pobrecito!!"* And it was his business to present him to the King.

The King shook his head when he saw the shepherd-staff in his hand and the shepherd-pouch hanging from his belt, and he said: "A shepherd's life is better than no life at all. Better go back to your flocks."

But the shepherd was as rich in stubbornness as he was poor in learning. He insisted he must answer the riddle. So the Infanta came and danced with the tambourine and the King laughed and said his rhyme:

"Belita—Felipa—they dance well together—
Belita—Felipa; now answer me whether
You know this Felipa—this *animalita*.
If you answer right, then you marry Belita."

The shepherd strode over and took the tambourine from the hand of the Infanta. He felt the skin carefully, carefully. To himself he said: "I know sheep and I know goats; and it isn't either.

"Can't you guess?" whispered the black beetle from his pouch.

"No," said the shepherd.

"Let me out," said the little ant; "perhaps I can tell you what it is." So the shepherd unfastened the pouch and La Hormiguita crawled out, unseen by the court. She crawled all over the tambourine and came back whispering, "You can't fool me. I'd know a flea anywhere, any size."

"Don't take all day," shouted the King. "Who is Felipa?"

"She's a flea," said the shepherd.

Then the court was in a flutter.

"I don't want to marry a shepherd," said the Infanta.

"You shan't," said the King.

"I'm the one to say 'shan't,' " said the shepherd.

"I will grant you any other favor," said the Infanta.

"I will grant you another," said the King.

"It was a long journey here, walking," said the shepherd. "I would like a cart to ride home in."

"And two oxen to draw it," whispered the black beetle.

"And two oxen to draw it," repeated the shepherd.

"You shall have them," said the King.

"And what shall I give you?" asked the Infanta.

"Tell her you want your pouch filled with gold," whispered Ratonperez.

"That's little enough," said the Infanta.

But while the royal groom was fetching the cart and oxen; and the lord of the exchequer was fetching a bag of gold; Ratonperez was gnawing a hole in the pouch. When they came to pour in the gold, it fell through as fast as water, so that all around the feet of the shepherd it rose like a shining yellow stream.

"That's a lot of gold," said the King at last.

"It's enough," said the shepherd. He took his

cart, filled it with the gold, drove back to the high-lands of Castile. He married a shepherd's daughter, who never had to do anything but sit in a rocking-chair and fan herself all day. And that's a contented life, you might say—for anyone who likes it.

Take hundreds of pins and chop off each head,
Put them on a large platter the color of lead;
Turn it upside-down; they'll not scatter about.
The day shuts them in; the night lets them out.
(Stars).

THE *Arabe* DUCK

WELL, THEN—once there was a duck who thought himself very wise and very important.

He came into Spain with the Arabs, which was a long time ago. That is why he was called the *Arabe* duck.

He settled in Valencia because he found many waterways there. There were ponds—big ones, small ones, and ones in between. He picked out one for himself that was in between and said: "No other duck shall live here, so there will always be plenty for me to eat."

The *Arabe* duck fared well. Fish abounded. All he had to do was to go in for them, head down, tail up. "They are stupid, those fish. It is a fine thing to be wise and clever as I am." That *Arabe* duck was a boaster.

No one shared the pond with him but the fishes, a few silly snails, and an old crab. How long the crab had been there, nobody knew. He was slow and stupid and minded his own business. He never disputed with the *Arabe* duck who owned the pond; so they got on splendidly together.

In time the duck grew old, less agile, more boastful. He tried to dive and prune his feathers and dart across the water with his customary vigor; but he only did it when the crab was about, to notice him. He had a hard time catching fish enough to satisfy his hunger. He would dive for them and they would be gone before he could get them. His dinners grew scantier, farther apart. One night he went to his bed in the rushes, hungry.

That night he was afraid—afraid. "I must use my wits," he said aloud to himself. "There must be some way to catch those fish without working so hard. And one grows always older—never younger."

By another springtime the *Arabe* duck had grown gaunt—tottering; not so much from age as for the want of a good meal. Often he thought: "A thousand molestations on those fish! The younger generations are quicker, less stupid than the old. I must think up a scheme of catching them off their guard."

At last he had an idea—excellent—stupendous! He said to the crab: "Señor Crab, I am wise. I can read the stars."

"Can you, really!" said the crab. "I didn't know the stars could write anything down for anybody to read."

"Don't talk nonsense," said the *Arabe* duck. "What I mean is quite different." He didn't explain why it was different, because he didn't know. But he had heard the Arabian astrologers talk about reading the stars and it sounded very wise and important. "Perhaps," he went on, "you would like to know what I have read."

"I would," said the crab, "if it's interesting."

"It is and it concerns all of us."

"What do you mean by 'all of us?' "

"Why, you, me and the fishes. You see, there is to be a great drought. There will be no rain. Everything is going to dry up. Only the big ponds—the very big ones will remain."

"Que lástima! That sounds bad."

"It will be unless we find quickly a bigger pond to live in."

"That is all very well for you. You walk—you fly. You can go wherever you please. But I have to stay here; so do the fishes."

"Not at all," said the *Arabe* duck, putting on a look of great benevolence. "I will carry you all. You go and tell the fish to swim close to the shore where I can pick them up quite easily. One by one I will take them across the *vega* to the first big pond, where they will be quite safe—oh, very safe."

So the crab told the fishes. After that every day was a feastday for the *Arabe* duck. All he had to do was to wade in from the beach; and the fish came swimming straight for his open bill. So afraid they were of being caught by the drought. The *Arabe* duck would handle them, each one, so gently; carry them beyond sight of the pond, gulp them down and come back for more. He grew fat and important again.

Now, the crab was stupid; but he had eyes at the back of his head. He saw the duck that had been starved grow sleek and plump. He saw the fish disappear and he asked himself—where? The *Arabe* duck became less and less careful. He grabbed for the fishes; he went only a little distance before he gobbled them down. One day he came back before he had completely swallowed the last one. The crab saw plainly the tail still hanging between the duck's bill.

"So, that is that," said the crab. "One does not grow fat on just walking." And aloud to the *Arabe* duck he said: "I, too, have read the stars. They tell me it is time that I went to the big pond. Señor, carry me there, for I shall be a hundred years walking it."

"And how shall I carry you?"

"This way. Let me put my big claw around your neck; take my little claw in your bill. In that way it will be easy."

The *Arabe* duck came close—close. He took in his bill the little claw, and lifted. Quickly the crab swung the big, the strong, the cutting claw aloft and clamped it tight around the neck of the *Arabe* duck. In a voice that bubbled softly the crab spoke. "There is more that I have read in the stars. They tell me that the fish have all gone into the very big pond of your stomach and that it is time to shut off the road leading to it. So!"

That was the end of the *Arabe* duck; and a good end, too; if you ask me or the crab or the fishes.

CLEVER—CLEVER—CLEVER

ONCE THERE WAS a farmer who thought *he* was a very clever man—and—

Once there was a bear who thought *he* was a very clever bear—and—

Once there was a fox who thought *she* was a very clever fox—and—

You shall soon see—
Which was the clever one of all three.

One day the farmer was plowing a field, making it ready to plant wheat. Oxen pulled the plow. They were too fat, too lazy. They went slower than the tortoise in summer or the toad in winter.

"*Arre,* lazy ones! Get alive both of you. I might as well have two dead oxen drawing my plow," the farmer grumbled. Then he tried frightening them: "Go faster—go faster—or I will give one of you to the bear to eat."

Now the bear was passing nearby. He was hungry—hungry. He heard what the farmer was saying. He crossed the field and said: "Farmer—you have made a fine promise. I am here to see that you keep it. Give me one of your oxen for my dinner."

The farmer did not wish to be caught this way by the bear, who he thought was stupid compared to himself. So he said: "Yes, yes, these two lazy ones are no better than dead. I am going to give you one to eat presently; but first I must finish plowing the field. Agreed?"

"Agreed. I will take it easy while you plow." And the bear went and laid himself down under the farmer's cart. There he went fast asleep.

Soon came the fox from the woods. She crossed the field on stealthy feet. "Farmer, I saw you and the bear speaking together. I saw him go quietly and lay himself down out of the sun. I am curious. What had you to say to one another?"

"He has caught me in a bad trap. When I finish plowing I must give him one of these oxen to eat."

"I have good wits," laughed the fox. "Will you give me a fat hen to eat if I save your ox for you?"

"One hen! I will give that hen and all the chickens I have."

"Agreed. Now give me your coat and hat. With them I will pretend I am a hunter. I will hide behind the rock at the top of the field and when I put up my head and call: 'Señor Farmer!' you must answer: 'Señor Hunter, what do you want?' "

The fox put on the coat and hat. She found a stick and laid it over her shoulder like a fowling-piece. She hid behind the rock so that only the hat, the shoulders and the stick showed. Then she called: "Señor Farmer!"

"Señor Hunter, what do you want?"

"I want to know what that is hiding under your cart. Is it something I can take a pot at?"

The bear had wakened at the shouting voices. He had heard everything. He was frightened—frightened—scared out of those fine wits of his. "Shout back to him that I am a piece of lumber," whispered the bear in a little voice.

"That is a piece of lumber," shouted the farmer.

"Señor Farmer!"

"Señor Hunter, what do you want?"

"What are you doing with the lumber?"

"Tell him you are taking it home to mend your barn with," answered the bear.

"I am taking it home to mend my barn with," shouted the farmer.

"Señor Farmer!"

"Señor Hunter, what do you want?"

"Why don't you put it in your cart, then?"

"Put me in your cart," said the bear.

The farmer tugged and pulled. He got the bear out from under the cart. He pulled and hoisted and got the bear in the cart.

"Señor Farmer!"

"Señor Hunter, what do you want?"

"In the country I come from when a person is hauling lumber in his cart he always ties it in with a strong rope."

"Tie me in," said the bear, "but not too tight."

The farmer tied him in; but not too loose.

"Señor Farmer!"

"Señor Hunter, what do you want?"

"In the country I come from they always thrust an ax well into the lumber when they are hauling it in a cart. That gives a handle to hold to so that there will be no chance of losing it on the road home."

"Thrust an ax into me but not too far," said the bear.

The farmer came close. He took up his ax. He let it fall straight onto the head of the bear. It killed him—like that!

The fox came running from behind the rock. "What wits I have! Here is your hat and coat. Now hurry home for that hen and those chickens."

The farmer, very thankful, went fast—fast. He said to his wife: "A fox now has saved me from having to kill one of the oxen—from being eaten myself by the bear. Go and fetch the hen and the eleven chickens. I must give them to her with my *muchas gracias.*"

The farmer's wife caught the hen. It was fat—fat. "It is a pity to have you eaten by nothing better than a sly fox. I will be clever and give her instead the dog and her puppies. She can eat them—if she likes."

The farmer's wife said nothing to the farmer. She filled the bag with the dog and her puppies. The farmer slung it over his shoulder and carried it to the fox. As he came close the fox shouted:

> "San Juan and San Bruno,
>   what carry you there?
> The fur of a dog
>   I smell in the air."

"A dog, nothing. It is the fat hen and eleven chickens—as I promised you." He slung the sack down beside the fox.

The fox laid her muzzle close and said:

> "San Pedro and San Juan,
>   my wits tell me when

I smell stable dog
　　or poultry-yard hen.
　　And this is *not* hen."

"Not hen!" The farmer was furious. "You dare to call an honest farmer a common cheat. Me—I have stripped the poultry-yard for you. Take the sack and begone."

So surely did the farmer speak of his honesty that he convinced the fox against the better judgment of her own nose. She took the sack, slung it over her shoulder and took the road to the mountain. Safe in the fastness of some rocks she opened the sack. Out jumped the dog, full speed after the fox, who cried as she ran:

"Good measure—I see—
　　We have cheated—all three—
　　The farmer, the bear and myself,
　　Ay de mi!"

At the end of the day the dog gave up the chase and the fox found her lair. She stretched herself out between her paws and looking hard at them, she said: "Poor *patitas!* You have been treated badly, this day of days. You have been bruised by stones, cut by thorns; yet you have brought me safely to cover. What shall I do for you? Sunday at the thieves' market I will buy you some little silk shoes."

"What will you buy me?" asked her ears. "I have been torn by briers."

"I will buy you a pair of lovely earrings."

"What will you buy me?" asked her tail. "I have been bitten deep by the dog as he jumped."

"I will buy you nothing," said the fox. "But I will make you a promise. From now until doomsday I will hide you between my legs whenever I am taken by surprise. Are you satisfied?"

"Well satisfied."

MARY C. HATCH

13 Danish Tales
SELECTIONS

NUMBER **7**
SERIES ONE

THE GREAT BOOKS FOUNDATION   *Chicago*

published and distributed by

THE GREAT BOOKS FOUNDATION
a nonprofit corporation
307 North Michigan Avenue, Chicago, Illinois 60601

13 DANISH TALES

MISTRESS GOOD LUCK
AND DAME KNOW-ALL

ONE DAY two old crones met on the highway. They were Mistress Good Luck and Dame Know-All, and as they walked along together, Mistress Good Luck said to the other, "Which do you think is better, good luck or great learning?"

"To be sure, and it's great learning," said Dame Know-All, but of course Mistress Good Luck did not agree with her, and so they fell to arguing about the matter, and they argued this way and that till they came to a field where a young lad was plowing.

Then Mistress Good Luck said, "Dear Dame Know-All, please wish a wish upon the head of the boy we see plowing yonder, and give him great learning and great wisdom. But luck he shall have none of, and then we will see which 'tis better to have, a bit of luck or a bit of learning."

"Very well," said Dame Know-All, and so she wished a wish upon the boy's head, and gave him wisdom and knowledge enough 'twould have made your head ache to carry it. Then she and Mistress

1

Good Luck moved on their way, and the lad went on with his plowing.

But not for long did he plow, for soon he began to feel how clever and wise he was, and after a short while, he threw down his reins and exclaimed, "I am so wise that there is nothing in the world I do not know, and now I am going to town and make myself a fortune." And there and then he skipped out of the field and started on his way.

When he arrived in town, he decided that he would like to be a watchmaker, so he went to the royal watchmaker and asked for a place in his shop. But this worthy man said nay, for the boy's fingers looked rough and clumsy, and besides, he was sure to have an enormous appetite and eat everyone out of house and home.

But the young man begged and begged, giving weight to his words with money, and so the watchmaker finally changed his mind, and the boy was given a place in the shop.

Not long after this, the king sent for the royal watchmaker. "My good man," he said, "I want you to make me a wondrous clock. It must walk about by itself, and when I sit on my throne and say, 'Here sits your great and loving majesty,' it is to stop in front of me and bow low."

"But your majesty!" cried the royal watchmaker. "Such a clock can never be made."

"If it is what the king wishes, it can be done," said his royal highness. "And if you lack fingers nimble enough or a head clever enough for the task, then we shall find another watchmaker to fill your shoes." And with that, the king walked haughtily away.

Now the poor man was so upset by this order that he could neither sleep nor eat, and finally the young apprentice said, "Master, if you will but give me leave, I can make the king's clock just as he wishes, and better, too."

But the master would have none of it. "Away with your nonsense," he cried. " 'Tis I who must make the clock."

Still not one spring of it got put together, and so the apprentice said a second time, "Master, if you will but give me leave, I can make the king's clock just as he wishes, and better, too."

But again the master refused him, and gave him a resounding box on the ears. Still not a spring got made, and so the boy said a third time, "Master, if you will but give me leave, I can make the king's clock just as he wishes, and better, too."

And this time the master gave leave, and what is

more, the lad was allowed to work in a room of his own, and he could come and go when and how he pleased.

Now a month and a day went by in this fashion, and then the master paid the lad a call to see how the clock was progressing. But not a bit of it was to be seen anywhere! Instead, the walls were covered from top to bottom with drawings that were strange and curious.

"A fine state of affairs, I must say," cried the master. "You beg and you promise, but not one spring of a clock do I see!"

"Well, you'll see it soon enough," said the boy. " 'Tis the plans, and good plans indeed, that I've drawn on the wall. Just leave me to work in peace and quiet, master."

And so the master left the boy to his work, and another month and a day went by. Then the master called on the lad again, and this time the room was heaped with wheels and cogs and cogs and wheels, all of a strange and curious size. But not a bit of a clock was to be seen anywhere!

"What a rascal you are," cried the master. "Here you beg and you promise, but never a clock do you make."

"Never fear," said the lad. "You shall have your clock before you know it. These are the works, and fine works, too, that you see here. Just leave me to work in peace and quiet, master."

And so the master left him, and sure enough, before he knew it, the clock *was* ready, and set upon his table to prove its excellence. And excellent it was, and wondrous, too. The master played that he was the king, and as the clock walked about, he said to it, "Here sits your great and loving majesty," and the clock stopped in front of him and bowed as prettily as a young page, and then beat out the time.

"What a wonderful, wonderful clock," cried the master. "If I had not seen that it was made all of steel inside, I would say it had a real live head and a real warm heart. Walk and tick and bow again, little jewel of a clock." And so the wondrous clock was obliged to amuse the watchmaker and the apprentices for several long hours.

Shortly thereafter, the king sent for the clock, and so the royal watchmaker and the young apprentice took it to the palace, and it was tried out before the whole court, from the king and queen down to the least important noble. And so well did it perform, walking and ticking and daintily bowing, that the king was ready to burst with pleasure.

"What did I tell you?" he cried to the master. "A real royal watchmaker can make a real royal clock if he is really a royal watchmaker!"

Then the master had to confess that 'twas not he, but the apprentice lad who had constructed the wondrous clock that could walk, and tick, and bow like a man.

"Well," said the king, "a lad with such a clever head needn't stay an apprentice for long." And there and then he made the boy a page in the palace.

Now you must know that this same king had a daughter, and the cat had got her tongue as the old saying goes, and no one could persuade her to open her mouth and say a word. This distressed her father no end, for though a talking woman is sometimes a nuisance, a silent one is even worse, and one never knows yea or nay if he's pleased her. And so the king was bound and determined to cure the lass, and he proclaimed far and wide that if anyone could make her talk, the princess would be his, and half the kingdom, too. But he wanted no halfhearted tries, and so those who failed must lose their lives.

Many a young man tried, for 'tis well known how easily a woman talks, and 'tis not unpleasant to marry a princess and own half a kingdom. But alas, these fine young men all failed, for the princess could not be persuaded to say a word, and one by one, they lost their lives.

Finally word of the stubborn girl reached the

ears of the new page, and he decided to try his luck with her. Into her chamber he walked one morning, and without giving her so much as a glance, went up to her mirror.

"Good morning, little mirror," he said. "I want to tell you a story. But remember, 'tis only a story. Once upon a time three men went for a walk in the country. They were an artist, a tailor, and a teacher. Now, little mirror, when night came, they had to keep a fire burning to guard themselves from the wild animals, so it was decided that while two of them slept, the other one should tend the fire.

"It was the artist's turn first—but remember this is only a story, little mirror—and as his companions lay snoring, he looked about for something to keep him awake, and what should he find but a tiny baby hidden in the grass! Then the tailor awakened, and quick as a wink, he made a fine dress for the child. Then the teacher awakened, and in a trice he taught the baby to speak. Now, little mirror— though you must remember this is only a story—to whom did the baby belong, to the artist, or the tailor, or the teacher? Think hard, little mirror, but remember this is only a story."

Then the princess cried out, "It belonged to the artist, of course, for he found it." And she danced up and down with excitement.

"That is right, very right," cried the lad, and all

aquiver with excitement himself, he ran out the door to proclaim his success in making the princess talk.

But alas, alack, where should he run but straight into the arms of the king's hangmen, and as they had neither seen nor heard the princess and would believe nothing but their own eyes and ears, they called the lad's story a tall tale, and hustled him out to the courtyard to be hanged.

And dead as a herring the poor boy soon would have been, but just at that moment Mistress Good Luck and Dame Know-All came walking by and discovered his plight.

"Well," cried Mistress Good Luck, "just see what wisdom and learning have done for this poor boy! He stands on the gallows before half his life is run, and nothing but good fortune can save him."

"Then give it to him, and be quick about it," cried Dame Know-All.

"Very well," said Mistress Good Luck. "But then will you still say that great knowledge is better than good fortune?"

No indeed, Dame Know-All would not, and so Mistress Good Luck waved the wand of fortune over the courtyard, and that brought the princess running from the palace and straight into the arms of the young lad.

"If you hang this boy, you will hang yourselves," she cried. "He told me a wonderful story and made me talk, and now I want to marry him if he will accept my hand."

Well, the hangmen wanted to keep their own heads, gray and bald though they were, and as it was plain to be seen that the princess was talking again, they let the lad go at once. Then the boy accepted the hand of the princess quite willingly, and soon they were married with great pomp and splendor.

And they lived happily ever after, happily indeed, for the lad's good luck never deserted him, and the princess always said just the right thing, never too much and never too little.

THE PRINCESS WHO ALWAYS BELIEVED

WHAT SHE HEARD

ONCE UPON A TIME, there was a king who had an only daughter. Now she was young and fair, and sweet and kind, but she had one unfortunate fault. She always believed everything she heard, and that would never do, for there's many a falsehood floating about this great world, particularly in circles of state, and a princess must always know true from untrue. Finally the king proclaimed that anyone who could make his daughter say, "It's a lie," should have her hand in marriage and rule half the kingdom.

Well, what an easy thing all the courtiers thought this would be, for they had long practiced the art of twisting the truth! And so they all vied with each other to tell the princess such lies that even a servant girl would have blushed with shame to believe them. But not a word of protest did the princess make.

When a prince of high repute said, "The moon is made of green cheese," she answered with a sweet sigh, "How I should like to have it for lunch—sliced very thin, of course."

And when a duke of distinction said, "I can balance myself on the head of a pin," she answered prettily, "A remarkable juggler indeed!"

And so on and on it went, till all the courtiers had tried in vain, and then all the rich merchants' sons took their turn, and as they were even more skilled than the courtiers in the art of telling untruths, they each expected to win the fair princess.

But they had bad luck, too, and it looked as if the kingdom would go to rack and ruin when the king died and there was no one to rule but a princess who could not tell right from wrong.

Then one sunny day, word of the king's plight reached the end of the kingdom where there lived a poor woodcutter and his only son, Claus. Claus was well known for stretching the truth, and when he heard the news, he said to himself, "I'm just the lad for the princess," and then and there he put on his Sunday best, bid his parents good-bye, and hurried off to the palace.

The king put no faith in the lad, however. "What would a poor lad like you, living far from court and understanding little of the ways of the world, know about true and untrue?" he asked.

"Oh, we country folk are clever," boasted the

lad. "I, myself, am well known for stretching the truth."

"Well, you may try then," said the king. "But where courtiers and merchants' sons have failed, I do not expect a common man to win."

"Well, we shall see what we shall see," said Claus, and so he was introduced to the princess, and they went to walk in the kitchen gardens. Here there were cabbages growing, and by one of them Claus stopped and said, " 'Tis a large cabbage you have here."

"The king feeds many mouths," answered the princess.

"But your cabbages are nothing to compare with my father's," said Claus. "Once we were building a new barn and there were sixteen carpenters work-ing on it. But all of a sudden a storm came up, and it rained so hard that they ran for shelter under one of the cabbage leaves. Then, after a long time, one of the men poked his knife through the leaf to see if the storm was over, and so much water poured through that all the poor men were drowned in an instant."

"What a huge cabbage indeed!" said the prin-cess, and that closed the subject of cabbages.

But the young man was not to be disposed of in

this way. He walked the princess over to the palace barn, and he said, " 'Tis a good-sized barn you have here, and solidly built, too."

"A royal house must have a royal barn," said the princess.

"But this barn is nothing compared to my father's barn," boasted Claus. "Why, our barn is so immense that it takes a cow years and years to walk through it from one end to the other. In fact, she comes out so old, she is good for nothing but the glue factory."

"A large barn indeed!" said the princess mildly, and that was the end of the barn.

But it was not the end of Claus, and he walked the princess to the pasture where the king's sheep were grazing.

" 'Tis fine, fat sheep you have, and woolly, too," said the lad.

"The king must sleep warm of a winter's night," said the princess.

"But these sheep are nothing to compare with my father's sheep," said Claus. "Why, their tails are so large that we must tie them to heavy wagons to hold them up, and when the village wants a pot of good soup, all we need to do is cut off a bit of a tail and there is enough for a hundred people. And that is

not all! When these sheep are sheared, we have to
hire sixteen woodcutters to chop off the wool with
axes, and each sheep takes a month and a day."

"What big sheep indeed!" said the princess, and
that was the end of that.

And it would have been the end of Claus, too,
were he a courtier or a merchant's son. But the son
of a woodcutter was not to be daunted by such a
little thing as a wrong-minded princess, so he led
her to the king's chicken coops, and here he said,
"You grow beautiful chickens, so snowy white, and
full of fine cackling, too."

"The king's chickens have something to crow
about," said the princess.

"But they are not so fine as my father's," said the
boy. "Why, their feathers are so stiff and long that
they can be used for ships' masts, and their eggs are
so large they will make a meal for the whole village,
and then we can saw the shells in half and there we
will have two seaworthy boats. There's nothing
slow about the way our hens lay either—ten wagon-
loads a day, piled high as a castle wall, sometimes
even higher, if we don't keep our eyes open. Why,
one day we had a pile that reached up to the moon,
and I was on top of it. 'Well,' thought I, 'I'll soon
climb down,' but before I could make a move, the

load toppled over, and there was I, hanging onto the moon, with nothing underneath. And I would have been hanging there still, if I hadn't been a quick-witted lad and found a cobweb that I fastened to a tree and used as a rope so as to lower myself slowly downward. But the cobweb did not reach far enough, alas, and so I had to jump the last few miles. And where should I land but right in the middle of the church! The pastor was taking up a collection for the poor, and your father was there, sitting on the floor with an old nightcap on his head and his pockets stuffed with gold and silver. But when the plate came to him, he refused to give more than one piece of money to the poor. He stuck his nose in the air, that selfish old fellow—"

"Stop!" cried the princess. "It's a lie!" And her pretty face was scarlet with anger. "If you must know," she exclaimed haughtily, "my father never wears anything less than his best crown in the church, and he is not selfish. He has shared many a palace crumb with the poor."

"I daresay that is so," said Claus, the wood-cutter's son. "But little does it matter, for I've made you say, 'It's a lie!' and now we'll be wed in the finest style."

This the princess could not deny, and so they

were married with great pomp and splendor. And neither Claus nor anyone else ever told lies again —which was very right, of course, but sometimes a little dull, and set Claus to yawning. And once he yawned so wide that he almost swallowed a whole house and lot. But that, of course, is another story!

HANS HUMDRUM

THERE WAS ONCE a man who had a wife, a farm, and three small sons. The first son was named Peter, the second one Paul, and the last Hans, though he was nearly always called Hans Humdrum because everyone thought he was a little stupid.

Now the farmer was very poor, and so, as the boys grew up, they were sent out into the world to shift for themselves. Since Peter was the oldest, it was his turn to go first, and early one morning his mother gave him a loaf of bread and some butter, and he started on his way.

He had walked hardly a mile, however, when whom should he meet but a rich farmer driving along in fine style. The farmer stopped and he stopped, and the farmer said to him, "Where are you going, my boy?"

"Out to seek my fortune," said Peter.

"Then you have crossed the right path," said the farmer, "for I am in need of a young man like you. Would you care to come and serve me?"

"I would indeed," said Peter, "provided the wages are good enough."

"The wages are fair as fair," said the farmer. "A bushel of dollars for six months' work from now until the first cuckoo calls. But before you say yes, I must warn you that I expect my hired men to be hard working and obedient. They must be up in the morning when the cock crows and work till I tell them to stop."

"You will find me up at the crack of dawn," said Peter. "And I will work like a house afire."

"Very well," said the farmer. "But that is not all. I am a happy, cheerful man, and I do not like to have sour faces around me, so I make an agreement with my hired men that the first one of us who becomes angry shall have a sound thrashing. If I become angry first, I will pay the man his wages, and he may go, so much the richer. But if he is ill-tempered first, I give him no more than his whipping, and out he goes, so much the poorer."

Now Peter considered this a very strange agreement, so he thought it over before saying yea or nay. The farmer looked anything but cheerful, for he was the ugliest man Peter had ever seen. His eyes were tiny, no bigger than a shoe button, his mouth reached from ear to ear, and his nose was so long he could almost stumble over it. But still and all, the wages were nothing to be sneezed at, and as Peter considered himself a good-natured lad and not easily offended, he finally said yes, and agreed to work for the farmer. Then he climbed into the carriage, and away they went, riding in fine style toward the farmer's house.

It was evening when they arrived, and the master told Peter he must begin threshing first thing in the morning. Then he sent the lad to bed, and as it was late, he soon fell fast asleep.

Next morning at six the cock crowed, and in a flash Peter was up and out to the threshing, where he worked for more than an hour without stopping. Then he began to feel hungry, and he wondered when his master would call him to breakfast. But never a sound came from the big farmhouse, so on he worked another hour and still another, until he was too hungry to thresh one more kernel of grain. Then he put down his flail, and walking across the yard, entered his master's house.

Here sat the farmer, and his wife, and his many children, all looking as if they had just enjoyed a fine breakfast, but not a morsel of food was in sight.

"Are you hungry, Peter?" asked the farmer, winking and blinking and twinkling his eyes.

"Yes, of course I am hungry," cried Peter. "I had no supper last night and no breakfast this morning, and well I need food, for I have been threshing these last three hours."

"Look above the door, Peter," said the farmer who, truth to tell, was not really a farmer at all, but a dreadful troll. "Look above the door and see what is written there."

Peter looked, and what should he see but a sign that said, "No breakfast till tomorrow." This provoked the lad, but he well remembered the troll's agreement, so when the old fellow asked, "Are you angry, Peter?" he answered, "Indeed I am not angry," and went whistling back to the barn. Here, fortunately, he found some bread and butter left over from yesterday, and as he ate it, he said to himself, "Well, no need to worry today, things will be better tomorrow. My master is but putting me to a test." Then he threshed on till nightfall and went to bed and to sleep with an empty stomach.

The next day the cock crowed at four o'clock instead of six. But this did not trouble Peter. "The earlier we're up, the sooner we'll eat," he said, and hurrying into his clothes, he ran to his work in the barn. He threshed for an hour, then stopped, thinking his master must surely have breakfast ready by now. But no one called him in to eat.

He threshed on another hour, and then was too hungry to work any longer, so he put down his flail and went into the house. Everything was just as it had been the day before. There sat the master, and his wife, and his many children, all looking as if they had had a wonderful breakfast, but nowhere in sight was there a morsel for Peter.

The farmer grinned with his big mouth that ran from ear to ear, and he said, "Surely you are not hungry, Peter?"

"Indeed I am hungry," answered Peter. "Yesterday I had nothing to eat, and this morning I have worked two long hours without a crumb of food. I am very hungry. I am starved."

The farmer went on grinning. "Look at the writing above the door, Peter," he said. Peter looked up, and there he saw the very same words he had seen the day before, "No breakfast till tomorrow."

"This is tomorrow," cried Peter. "And I am tired of your foolishness. One cannot work without eating."

"And one should not forget his agreements," said the farmer. "You are angry, aren't you, Peter?"

Angry! Yes indeed, for this was no way for a master to treat his servants.

Then how the troll did laugh, and in less time than it can be told, Peter received a sound thrashing, and was tossed outside the gate, sore and bruised, and hardly able to walk away. It took him many days to get home, and then he was obliged to stay in bed for many more. And what was worse, his parents gave him no sympathy whatever. No doubt his master had only wished to put him to a test, they said, and for a bushel of dollars, he should have been willing to go hungry a week.

The parents then sent Paul out to seek his fortune, and early one morning away he started. He traveled a mile or so, and then whom should he meet but the same old troll farmer driving along as before in fine fashion.

"Where are you going, my lad?" asked the farmer.

"Out to seek my fortune," said Paul.

"Then you have crossed the right path, for I am in need of a young man like you," said the farmer. "Would you care to come and serve me?"

"I would indeed," said Paul, "provided the wages are fair enough."

The wages were fair as fair, a bushel of dollars for six months' work from now until the first cuckoo called. But before Paul said yes, he must know that the farmer liked only helpers who were obedient and hard working, and since he was also a very cheerful man, they must be cheerful, too. The farmer explained the agreement he always made with his men, that whoever was angry first should receive a sound thrashing and lose his wages to boot.

It was a strange agreement, Paul thought, but as he was a cheerful lad, he did not worry about it overlong. He said yes, he would work for the farmer, and so off they went at once, driving together in fine style toward the farmer's house.

They arrived at nightfall, and the farmer reminded Paul that he must be up when the cock crowed in the morning and work till he was told to stop. All this Paul promised to do, and then, as it was very late, he went straight to bed and fell fast asleep.

In the morning he was up at the crack of dawn and went straight to the threshing where he worked for several hours without a moment's stop. Then he began to feel hungry and wondered when the master would call him to breakfast. But never a sound did he hear, and after a time he grew so hungry that he could thresh no longer, so he put down his flail, and went across the yard to the house. There inside sat the farmer, and his wife, and his many children, all looking as if they had just finished a fine meal, but not a morsel of food was in sight for Paul. And when he asked about food, the farmer pointed to the words above the door, "No breakfast till tomorrow."

This provoked Paul, but he remembered the farmer's agreement, so he said, "Very well, master, tomorrow is not far away." And he went whistling back to the barn where, luckily, he found some bread and butter left over from yesterday. This he ate and then went on threshing grain till it was dark and time to go to bed.

The next morning he got up expecting to find a big breakfast waiting for him, but everything was just the same as the day before, and he worked from dawn to dark with not a bite to eat nor a sip to drink. The same thing happened the third day, too, and then Paul lost his patience, and when the farmer said, "But surely you are not angry, Paul!" he cried, "Indeed I am angry. For three days I have worked from dawn to dark, but not once have I had a bite to eat or a sip to drink. I am angry to bursting."

"Well, that is a sad state of affairs," said the farmer, "for you remember our agreement." Then quick as a wink poor Paul got his thrashing and found himself outside the farmer's gate. He was bruised and sore, and it took him many days to return home, and many more in bed before he was well again.

Now the poor old folks had two sons to take care of and none to seek his fortune, for they did not think Hans Humdrum could be sent out into the world alone. But Hans was of another mind, and while his parents nursed the two older boys and cursed the cruel master, he did a good bit of thinking. Then one morning, without saying a word to anyone, he slipped out of the house and up the highway, bent on making his fortune, too.

He traveled a mile or so, and then, as luck would have it, he also met the old troll farmer with his long nose and his mouth that reached from ear to ear.

"Where are you going, my lad?" asked the farmer.

"Out to seek my fortune," said Hans.

"Then you have crossed the right path, for I am in need of a young man like you," said the farmer. "Would you care to come and serve me?"

"I would indeed," said Hans, "provided the wages are fair enough."

"The wages are fair as fair," said the farmer. "A bushel of dollars for six months' work from now until the first cuckoo calls. But you must be up in the morning with the cocks, and work till I tell you to stop. And I must warn you, too, that I am a cheerful man," said the farmer, and he went on to tell Hans the agreement he always made with his helpers.

"I am cheerful myself," said Hans when the farmer had finished. "And I know we will get along well together."

"Well, we shall see," laughed the farmer grinning from ear to ear. "Now hop into my wagon and we will be off."

This Hans did, and away they went, driving at a fast pace toward the master's farm. They arrived there late that evening and Hans went straight to bed and soon was fast asleep in the very room where his brothers had slept before him.

At six o'clock next morning the cock crowed, and Hans got up and went straight to the threshing. He worked for an hour, then stopped, expecting breakfast to be called. But not a sound came from the big house, so he went in to look for himself. There at the table sat the farmer, and his wife, and his many children, all looking as if they had just eaten a fine meal, but not a morsel was to be seen for Hans.

"Good morning," said the lad politely. "It is time for breakfast, is it not?"

"I wouldn't say that," said the farmer. "Have you read what is written above the door?"

Hans looked up and saw the same old sign, "No breakfast till tomorrow."

"Well, tomorrow is far ahead," he said. "We

can't worry about that until the time comes. Meanwhile I am a hungry lad."

"Then you may look to the rye for your food," laughed the farmer, and he sent Hans flying back to the grain. Here the poor lad worked on through the morning, saying nothing, but thinking much, and when dinnertime came, he filled a sack with rye and carried it to an innkeeper who lived near by.

"My master and I have agreed that I shall not eat at his house," said Hans, "but I am to look to the rye for my food. Will you feed me for this bushel of rye?"

"That I will do, and gladly," said the innkeeper, and there and then he served Hans a fine dinner, and filled his knapsack for the morrow. This made the lad feel better, and he soon was able to return to his work.

Several days passed in this fashion, and when the farmer asked Hans, "You are not angry, my lad?" he answered promptly, "And why should I be angry? I work well, and you have promised to give me breakfast in the morning."

On the fourth morning, when the farmer had again inquired, "You are not angry, Hans?" and Hans had replied, "Indeed I am not angry," the farmer continued, "But you have had nothing to eat for three whole days, and tomorrow never comes."

"But I have eaten," said Hans, "and well, too, thank you, for I followed your instruction to look to the rye for my food, and each day I exchange a bushel of rye with the innkeeper for a fine dinner and other provisions besides."

At this, the farmer's eyes almost bulged out of his head and his long mouth fell down to his chin.

"I hope master is not angry with me," said Hans innocently.

"By no means," said the farmer, trying very hard to look cheerful again. "But now you have done enough threshing and I have another task for you. I want you to plow some of the fields. My dog will go with you, and when he lies down you must start, and when he gets up you must stop, and if he comes home you must follow, no matter the path he may take."

Hans did as his master ordered, and when the dog lay down, he started to plow and worked till noon without stopping. Then he began to feel hungry, and he looked inquiringly at the dog. But that creature seemed in no hurry to leave, so he seized a whip and struck him soundly across the legs. At that, the dog was quite willing to go, and leaping up with a howl, he streaked across the field toward home. Hans then jumped down from the plow, undid the horses, and rode after the dog at a furious pace.

When they reached the house, the dog jumped over the garden fence, and Hans jumped the horses after him. However, they were not as nimble as the dog, and one of them fell and broke his leg, while the other one ran into a fence post. Neither could move now, and when the troll farmer ran out of his house and saw what had happened, he looked black as thunder.

But Hans said with a smile, "Surely you are not angry, master, for I was only obeying your orders. I am not to blame if the horses cannot jump over the fence as nimbly as a dog."

"I am not angry," said the troll. "Come in and have some dinner," and he tried very hard to smile from one end of his big mouth to the other. But it was difficult, for he was beginning to fear this boy who obeyed him so completely.

Hans had both dinner and supper, and the next morning the troll sent him out to tend the pigs. There were fifty of them, sleek and fat, and just ready for market.

"Let them go wherever they wish," said the troll. "Let them bury themselves in the mud if that's what they want."

"Yes indeed, master," said Hans, and he followed the pigs out of the yard.

The animals wandered slowly up the road, eating here and there, and Hans idly followed them until he met a couple of men who had been about the countryside buying cattle and swine.

"What fine pigs you have there," said the men to Hans.

"The best from here to yonder and back again," replied Hans.

"And would you be willing to sell them?" asked the men.

"I would indeed," answered Hans, "for a fine pig looks better on the table than on the hoof. I will sell all but this big one," and he pointed to an old sow. "She is intended as a present for the pastor."

"What a good lad to think of the pastor," said the buyers, and so they paid Hans well for the pigs, and a dollar extra besides. Then they drove east with their fine, fat swine, and Hans walked west with his one lone sow. He had his eye out for a marsh, and when he came to one, he let the pig bury herself in the mud until only her tail stood above the ground. Then he returned to the house.

"What has become of my pigs?" cried the troll when he saw that Hans was all alone.

"Master, master," Hans replied, "your pigs rooted themselves into the bog and all are lost except one old sow. I hung onto her tail and that is still above the mud, but all the rest are gone."

The troll shrieked and ran down to the bog. There he saw the tail of his one poor pig waving above the mud, and he reached down and tried to pull her out. But the tail slipped between his fingers, and down he, too, tumbled into the bog. When he pulled himself out again, wet and muddy, Hans said, "I hope you are not angry with me, master. I did only what you said to do."

"No, I am not angry," said the troll, but he did not smile, and he ran wildly about, looking for his lost pigs, which, alas, he could not find, for as Hans had explained, they were now far away.

Finally he gave up and went home, and when he saw his wife, he said, "What can I do to get rid of that wretched boy before he does away with everything I own? If only I could tell him how angry I am! Why did I make that foolish agreement?"

"Never fear," cried his wife. "We can easily get rid of him. He knows that his time is up when the first cuckoo calls, so we will play a trick on him. You cover me with tar and roll me in feathers till I look like a bird. Then help me up into the large apple tree, and there I will cry, 'Cuckoo, cuckoo,' until Hans thinks that the bird has really come and you can send him sailing."

"My, but you are a clever woman," exclaimed the troll, and he grinned for the first time in many days. "I will do exactly as you say." And with that he made ready for tomorrow's trick.

The next morning as Hans and the troll sat at the

table eating breakfast, they heard the loud call of a cuckoo.

"Well, what a surprise," exclaimed the troll. "I do believe the cuckoo has come."

"Then I must see him," cried Hans. "I have always wanted to have a look at the first summer cuckoo." And he jumped up and ran outside to the garden. There he saw the strangest-looking bird he had ever laid eyes on in all his life, and picking up a sharp stone, he threw it straight at the creature's head. Down she fell, stone dead, and Hans cried to the troll, "Come, master, come and look at this strange bird."

Now of course it was not really a bird that Hans had killed, but the troll's old woman, and when he rushed out and saw what had happened, he was so angry that sparks flew from his eyes and his voice roared like thunder.

"I hope master is not angry," said Hans softly.

"Indeed I am angry," cried the troll. "You have sold my rye, you have ruined my horses, and lost my swine, and now you have killed my wife. I could tear you limb from limb, you scoundrel." And he shook like a hurricane, he was so full of rage and fury.

"Well," said Hans quietly, "that is indeed sad, for now I must deal with you according to the terms of our agreement." And he seized the troll and thrashed him until the old fellow could not lift a finger. Then he ran gaily into the house, took the bushel of dollars which was due him and returned home to his parents and brothers. And here they all lived happily ever after, and neither saw nor heard any more of the troll.

NOTES

CHARLES PERRAULT

Fairy Tales

NUMBER 8
SERIES ONE

THE GREAT BOOKS FOUNDATION   *Chicago*

published and distributed by

THE GREAT BOOKS FOUNDATION
a nonprofit corporation
307 North Michigan Avenue, Chicago, Illinois 60601

FAIRY TALES

THE MASTER CAT
Or: Puss-in-Boots

A MILLER died, leaving as sole riches to his three sons his mill, his donkey, and his cat. The estate was easily shared out; neither the lawyer nor the notary was called in. They would soon have gobbled up the meagre inheritance. The eldest son had the mill, the second the donkey, and the youngest only the cat.

The last was inconsolable at having such a poor share.

'My brothers,' he said, 'can earn a decent living if they combine together. But when I have eaten my cat and made myself a muff from its skin, I shall just have to starve.'

The Cat, who heard these words but pretended not to, said in calm, confident tones:

'Do not worry, master. Just give me a sack and have a pair of boots made so that I can go in the brambles, and you will find that you are not so badly off after all.'

Although the Cat's master did not put much faith in this suggestion, he had seen him perform such ingenious tricks to catch rats and mice, such as hanging upside down by his feet, or lying in the flour-bin pretending to be dead, that he decided that it might be worth trying.

When the Cat had the things he had asked for, he buckled the boots on smartly, slung the sack over his shoulder and, holding the cords with his fore-paws, went off to a warren where there were large numbers of rabbits.

He placed some bran and sow-thistles in his sack and, stretching himself out on the ground as though he were dead, waited for some young rabbit, still unused to the wiles of this world, to hop into the sack to get what was in it.

He had hardly lain down when his trick worked. A silly young rabbit jumped into the sack and the Master Cat quickly pulled the cords and caught and killed him without mercy.

Swelling with pride in this achievement, he went to the palace and asked to speak to the King. He was taken up to His Majesty's apartments and, as he came in, he made a low bow and said:

'Sire, here is a rabbit which My Lord the Marquis of Carabas' (that was the name which he had decided to give his master) 'has instructed me to offer you on his behalf.'

'Tell your master,' said the King, 'that We thank him and that he gives Us great pleasure.'

Another day he went and hid in a cornfield, again with his open sack, and when two partridges flew in, he pulled the cords and caught them both. He presented these to the King, as he had done with the rabbit. The King again accepted the gift with pleasure and gave him some drinking-money.

The Cat went on in this way for two or three months, taking game to the King every so often 'from his master's hunting-grounds.' One day he heard that the King was to go for a drive along the river-bank with his daughter, the loveliest princess in the world, so he said to his master:

'If you will follow my advice, your fortune is made. All you have to do is to bathe in the river at the spot which I will show you, and leave the rest to me.'

The Marquis of Carabas did as his Cat told him, without knowing what would come of it. While he was bathing, the King came by and the Cat began to cry at the top of his voice:

'Help! Help! My Lord the Marquis of Carabas is drowning!'

The King looked out of the carriage window and, recognizing the Cat which had so often brought him game, he ordered his guards to go quickly to the help of My Lord the Marquis of Carabas.

As the poor Marquis was being pulled out of the river, the Cat went up to the carriage and told the King that, while his master was bathing, some thieves had made off with his clothes, although he had shouted 'Stop thief!' at the top of his voice. The rascal had really hidden them under a big stone.

The King immediately ordered the officers of his wardrobe to go and fetch one of his finest suits for My Lord the Marquis of Carabas. The King was kindness itself to him and, since the fine clothes which he had been given set off his good looks— for he was handsome and well-built—the King's daughter took an immediate liking to him; and, by the time he had thrown her a few appreciative but most respectful glances, she had fallen madly in love.

The King insisted that he should get into the carriage and accompany them on the drive. De-lighted to see that his plan was beginning to suc-ceed, the Cat ran ahead until he came to some peasants who were mowing a meadow.

'Dear good mowers,' he said, 'if you do not tell the King that the meadow you are mowing belongs to my Lord the Marquis of Carabas, I will have you all chopped up into mincemeat.'

The King did not fail to ask them whose meadow they were mowing.

'It belongs to My Lord the Marquis of Carabas,' they answered in chorus, for the Cat's threat had terrified them.

'You have a fine piece of land there,' said the King to the Marquis of Carabas.

'As you see, Sire,' answered the Marquis. 'It gives a wonderful crop every year.'

The Master Cat, still running ahead, came to some harvesters and said to them:

'Dear good harvesters, if you do not say that these cornfields belong to My Lord the Marquis of Carabas, I will have you all chopped up into mincemeat.'

The King, coming up a moment later, asked who was the owner of all these cornfields which he saw.

'They belong to My Lord the Marquis of Carabas,' cried the harvesters, and the King again congratulated the Marquis. The Cat, keeping ahead of the carriage, said the same thing to all the people whom he met, and the King was astonished at the vast estates of the Marquis of Carabas.

At last the Cat reached a fine castle whose master was an ogre. He was the richest ogre of them all, for all the land through which the King had passed belonged to him. The Cat, having first found out who this ogre was and what he could do, asked to speak to him, saying that he could not pass so near to his castle without having the honour of calling in to pay his respects.

The ogre received him as civilly as an ogre can and told him to take a seat.

'I have heard,' said the Cat, 'that you have the power of changing yourself into all kinds of animals; for example, that you can turn into a lion, or an elephant.'

'That is so,' said the ogre gruffly, 'and to show you, I will turn into a lion.'

The Cat was so scared at seeing a lion before him that he sprang up on to the roof, not without some danger and difficulty, because his boots were not suitable for walking on the tiles.

After some time, the Cat saw that the ogre had gone back to his original shape, so he came down, admitting that he had had quite a fright.

'I have also heard,' he went on, 'that you have the power to take on the shape of the smallest animals, for instance to turn into a rat or a mouse. I must admit that I think that is quite impossible.'

'Impossible!' roared the ogre, 'You shall see!'

And he immediately turned into a mouse, which began to scurry across the floor. As soon as the cat saw it, he sprang upon it and ate it.

Meanwhile the King came in sight of the ogre's

fine castle and said that he would like to go in. The Cat, hearing the sound of the carriage on the draw-bridge, ran out and said to the King:

'Welcome, Your Majesty, to the castle of the Marquis of Carabas.'

'What, My Lord Marquis,' said the King, 'this castle is yours, too? Nothing could be finer than this courtyard and these buildings round it. Let Us see inside, please.'

The Marquis offered his hand to the young Princess and, following the King, they went up the steps to the great hall. There they found a magnificent feast which the ogre had prepared for some of his friends who had been invited for that same day, but had not dared to come in when they heard that the King was there.

The King was delighted with all the virtues of My Lord the Marquis of Carabas, while as for his daughter, she was in raptures about him. Seeing his vast possessions and having drunk a few draughts of wine, the King said:

'You have only to say the word, My Lord Marquis, and you can become our son-in-law.'

With a low bow the Marquis accepted the honour which the King proposed, and he was married to the Princess on that same day. The Cat became a great lord and from then on only hunted mice as a relaxation.

MORAL

Inherited wealth is all very fine
As it passes on down the family line,
But young men who really want to get on
Could learn from the cat of the miller's son
      That smartness pays
      Better nowadays.

SECOND MORAL

If, in a matter of hours, by a miller's son
The heart of a monarch's daughter can be won,
Till she gazes at him with languid, lovelorn eyes,
The reason might be that youth, good looks and
      dress
Have a part to play in promoting love's success
Whose importance it would be a great mistake
      to despise.

CINDERELLA

Or: The Little Glass Slipper

ONCE THERE WAS a nobleman who took as his second wife the proudest and haughtiest woman imaginable. She had two daughters of the same character, who took after their mother in everything. On his side, the husband had a daughter who was sweetness itself; she inherited this from her mother, who had been the most kindly of women.

No sooner was the wedding over than the stepmother showed her ill-nature. She could not bear the good qualities of the young girl, for they made her own daughters seem even less likeable. She gave her the roughest work of the house to do. It was she who washed the dishes and the stairs, who cleaned out Madam's room and the rooms of the two Misses. She slept right at the top of the house, in an attic, on a lumpy mattress, while her sisters slept in panelled rooms where they had the most modern beds and mirrors in which they could see themselves from top to toe. The poor girl bore everything in patience and did not dare to complain to her father. He would only have scolded her, for he was entirely under his wife's thumb.

When she had finished her work, she used to go into the chimney-corner and sit down among the cinders, for which reason she was usually known in the house as Cinderbottom. Her younger stepsister, who was not so rude as the other, called her Cinderella. However, Cinderella, in spite of her ragged clothes, was still fifty times as beautiful as her sisters, superbly dressed though they were.

One day the King's son gave a ball, to which everyone of good family was invited. Our two young ladies received invitations, for they cut quite a figure in the country. So there they were, both feeling very pleased and very busy choosing the clothes and the hair-styles which would suit them best. More work for Cinderella, for it was she who ironed her sisters' underwear and goffered their linen cuffs. Their only talk was of what they would wear.

'I,' said the elder, 'shall wear my red velvet dress and my collar of English lace.'

'I,' said the younger, 'shall wear just my ordinary skirt; but, to make up, I shall put on my gold-embroidered cape and my diamond clasp, which is quite out of the common.'

The right hairdresser was sent for to supply double-frilled coifs, and patches were bought from the right patch-maker. They called Cinderella to ask her opinion, for she had excellent taste. She made useful suggestions and even offered to do their hair for them. They accepted willingly.

While she was doing it, they said to her:

'Cinderella, how would you like to go to the ball?'

'Oh dear, you are making fun of me. It wouldn't do for me.'

'You are quite right. It would be a joke. People would laugh if they saw a Cinderbottom at the ball.'

Anyone else would have done their hair in knots for them, but she had a sweet nature, and she finished it perfectly. For two days they were so excited that they ate almost nothing. They broke a good dozen laces trying to tighten their stays to make their waists slimmer, and they were never away from their mirrors.

At last the great day arrived. They set off, and Cinderella watched them until they were out of sight. When she could no longer see them, she began to cry. Her godmother, seeing her all in tears, asked what was the matter.

'If only I could . . . If only I could . . .' She was weeping so much that she could not go on.

Her godmother, who was a fairy, said to her: 'If only you could go to the ball, is that it?'

'Alas, yes,' said Cinderella with a sigh.

'Well,' said the godmother, 'be a good girl and I'll get you there.'

She took her into her room and said: 'Go into the garden and get me a pumpkin.'

Cinderella hurried out and cut the best she could find and took it to her godmother, but she could not understand how this pumpkin would get her to the ball. Her godmother hollowed it out, leaving only the rind, and then tapped it with her wand and immediately it turned into a magnificent gilded coach.

Then she went to look in her mouse-trap and found six mice all alive in it. She told Cinderella to raise the door of the trap a little, and as each mouse came out she gave it a tap with her wand and immediately it turned into a fine horse. That made a team of six horses, each of a fine mouse-coloured grey.

While she was wondering how she would make a coachman, Cinderella said to her:

'I will go and see whether there is a rat in the rat-trap, we could make a coachman of him.'

'You are right,' said the godmother. 'Run and see.'

Cinderella brought her the rat-trap, in which there were three big rats. The fairy picked out one of them because of his splendid whiskers and, when she had touched him, he turned into a fat coachman, with the finest moustaches in the district.

Then she said: 'Go into the garden and you will find six lizards behind the watering-can. Bring them to me.'

As soon as Cinderella had brought them, her godmother changed them into six footmen, who got up behind the coach with their striped liveries, and stood in position there as though they had been doing it all their lives.

Then the fairy said to Cinderella:

'Well, that's to go to the ball in. Aren't you pleased?'

'Yes. But am I to go like this, with my ugly clothes?'

Her godmother simply touched her with her wand and her clothes were changed in an instant into a dress of gold and silver cloth, all sparkling with precious stones. Then she gave her a pair of glass slippers, most beautifully made.

So equipped, Cinderella got into the coach; but her godmother warned her above all not to be out after midnight, telling her that, if she stayed at the ball a moment later, her coach would turn back into a pumpkin, her horses into mice, her footmen into lizards, and her fine clothes would become rags again.

She promised her godmother that she would leave the ball before midnight without fail, and she set out, beside herself with joy.

The King's son, on being told that a great princess whom no one knew had arrived, ran out to welcome her. He handed her down from the coach and led her into the hall where his guests were. A sudden silence fell; the dancing stopped, the violins ceased to play, the whole company stood fascinated by the beauty of the unknown princess. Only a low murmur was heard: 'Ah, how lovely she is!' The King himself, old as he was, could not take his eyes off her and kept whispering to the Queen that it was a long time since he had seen such a beautiful and charming person. All the ladies were absorbed in noting her clothes and the way her hair was dressed, so as to order the same things for themselves the next morning, provided that fine enough materials could be found, and skilful enough craftsmen.

The King's son placed her in the seat of honour, and later led her out to dance. She danced with such grace that she won still more admiration. An excellent supper was served, but the young Prince was too much occupied in gazing at her to eat anything. She went and sat next to her sisters and treated them with great courtesy, offering them oranges and lemons which the Prince had given her. They were astonished, for they did not recognize her.

While they were chatting together, Cinderella heard the clock strike a quarter to twelve. She curtsied low to the company and left as quickly as she could.

As soon as she reached home, she went to her godmother and, having thanked her, said that she would very much like to go again to the ball on the next night—for the Prince had begged her to come back. She was in the middle of telling her godmother about all the things that had happened, when the two sisters came knocking at the door. Cinderella went to open it.

'How late you are!' she said, rubbing her eyes and yawning and stretching as though she had just woken up (though since they had last seen each other she had felt very far from sleepy).

'If you had been at the ball,' said one of the sisters, 'you would not have felt like yawning. There was a beautiful princess there, really ravishingly beautiful. She was most attentive to us. She gave us oranges and lemons.'

Cinderella could have hugged herself. She asked them the name of the princess, but they replied that no one knew her, that the King's son was much troubled about it, and that he would give anything in the world to know who she was. Cinderella smiled and said to them:

'So she was very beautiful? Well, well, how lucky you are! Couldn't I see her? Please, Miss Javotte, do lend me that yellow dress which you wear about the house.'

'Really,' said Miss Javotte, 'what an idea! Lend one's dress like that to a filthy Cinderbottom! I should have to be out of my mind.'

Cinderella was expecting this refusal and she was very glad when it came, for she would have been in an awkward position if her sister had really lent her her frock.

On the next day the two sisters went to the ball, and Cinderella too, but even more splendidly dressed than the first time. The King's son was constantly at her side and made love to her the whole evening. The young girl was enjoying herself so much that she forgot her godmother's warning. She heard the clock striking the first stroke of midnight when she thought that it was still hardly eleven. She rose and slipped away as lightly as a roe-deer. The Prince followed her, but he could not catch her up.

One of her glass slippers fell off, and the Prince picked it up with great care.

Cinderella reached home quite out of breath, with no coach, no footmen, and wearing her old clothes. Nothing remained of all her finery, except one of her little slippers, the fellow to the one which she had dropped. The guards at the palace gate were asked if they had not seen a princess go out. They answered that they had seen no one go out except a very poorly dressed girl, who looked more like a peasant than a young lady.

When the two sisters returned from the ball, Cinderella asked them if they had enjoyed themselves again, and if the beautiful lady had been there. They said that she had, but that she had run away when it struck midnight, and so swiftly that she had lost one of her glass slippers, a lovely little thing. The Prince had picked it up and had done nothing but gaze at it for the rest of the ball, and undoubtedly he was very much in love with the beautiful person to whom it belonged.

They were right, for a few days later the King's son had it proclaimed to the sound of trumpets that he would marry the girl whose foot exactly fitted the slipper. They began by trying it on the various princesses, then on the duchesses and on all the ladies of the Court, but with no success. It was

brought to the two sisters, who did everything possible to force their feet into the slipper, but they
could not manage it. Cinderella, who was looking
on, recognized her own slipper, and said laughing:
'Let me see if it would fit me!'

Her sisters began to laugh and mock at her. But
the gentleman who was trying on the slipper looked
closely at Cinderella and, seeing that she was very
beautiful, said that her request was perfectly reasonable and that he had instructions to try it on
every girl. He made Cinderella sit down and, rais-
ing the slipper to her foot, he found that it slid on
without difficulty and fitted like a glove.

Great was the amazement of the two sisters, but
it became greater still when Cinderella drew from
her pocket the second little slipper and put it on her
other foot. Thereupon the fairy godmother came in
and, touching Cinderella's clothes with her wand,
made them even more magnificent than on the pre-
vious days.

Then the two sisters recognized her as the lovely
princess whom they had met at the ball. They flung
themselves at her feet and begged her forgiveness
for all the unkind things which they had done to
her. Cinderella raised them up and kissed them,
saying that she forgave them with all her heart and
asking them to love her always. She was taken to

the young Prince in the fine clothes which she was wearing. He thought her more beautiful than ever and a few days later he married her. Cinderella, who was as kind as she was beautiful, invited her two sisters to live in the palace and married them, on the same day, to two great noblemen of the Court.

MORAL

Beauty in a girl is a priceless treasure;
Simply to admire it gives endless pleasure.
But one quality is even more precious:
It's the gift that is known as being gracious.

Cinderella's godmother, as we have seen,
Drilled her in this from the head to the toes,
To such perfection that she made her a queen,
(So upon this tale the moralizing goes).

Girls, this gift is better than the latest hair-style;
To capture a heart, beyond question to win it,
Graciousness is the gift with true magic in it.
With a frown you get nothing, you get all with a
smile.

SECOND MORAL

To have wit and courage
Is a great advantage;
Good breeding, good sense
And similar talents
Are all heaven-sent.

But, though they are good,
These alone will not do;
To succeed as you should
You need godmothers, too.

RICKEY WITH THE TUFT

ONCE THERE WAS a Queen who gave birth to a son who was so ugly and misshapen that for some time they doubted whether he was human. A fairy who was present at his birth declared that he was certain to be lovable because of his quickness of understanding. She added that, by virtue of the power which she had just given him, he would be able to bestow as much understanding as he himself possessed on the person whom he loved most.

All this only slightly consoled the poor Queen, who was distressed at having brought such an ugly brat into the world. It is true that, as soon as the child began to speak, he said so many pretty things and there was something so delightful in all his ways, that everyone was charmed by him. I forgot to say that he was born with a little tuft of hair on his head and for that reason was called Rickey with the Tuft, Rickey being the family name.

Seven or eight years later, the Queen of a neighbouring kingdom gave birth to twin daughters. The first who came into the world was as beautiful as the day. The Queen was so delighted that those around her feared that her excessive joy might do her some harm. The same fairy who had been at the birth of Rickey with the Tuft was there too, and, in order to calm the Queen, she assured her that the little princess would be completely lacking in understanding and would be as stupid as she was beautiful.

This greatly mortified the Queen, but a few moments later she had a much bigger disappointment, for when the second twin was born it proved to be extremely ugly.

'Do not distress yourself so much, Madam,' said the fairy. 'Your daughter will have other compensations. She will be so clever that people will hardly notice that she has no beauty.'

'I hope so with all my heart,' said the Queen. 'But is there no way of giving a little wit to the elder, who is so beautiful?'

'I can do nothing for her, Madam, in the way of wit,' said the fairy, 'but I can do anything in the way of beauty. So, as there is nothing that I would not do to please you, I will give her the power of being able to bestow good looks on the person whom she likes best.'

As the two daughters grew up, their good qualities grew with them, and the whole kingdom ad-

mired the beauty of the elder and the intelligence of
the younger. It is also true that their bad qualities
increased considerably with age. The younger
seemed to grow uglier every day, the elder more
and more stupid. Either she made no reply when
spoken to, or else she gave a foolish answer. Besides
that, she was so clumsy that she could not arrange
four vases along the mantelpiece without breaking
one of them, or drink a glass of water without spill-
ing half of it over her clothes.

Beauty is a great asset to a young girl, yet, wherever they happened to go, the younger was nearly
always more in demand than her sister. At first
people crowded round the beautiful one, just to see
her and admire her, but soon they moved to the
clever one, to listen to all the amusing things which
she had to say. After a quarter of an hour they were
all gathered round the younger one, while the elder
had no one near her at all.

Although she was very stupid, the elder noticed
this and she would willingly have given all her
beauty to have half her sister's wit. The Queen, for
all her wise heart, could not help scolding her sometimes for her stupidity, and this reduced the poor
Princess almost to despair.

One day when she had gone alone into a wood to
lament her misfortunes, she saw walking towards

her a little man of ugly and unprepossessing appearance, but splendidly dressed. It was the young prince Rickey with the Tuft, who had fallen in love with the pictures of her which were circulated, and had left his father's kingdom in the hope of meeting her and talking to her.

Delighted to find her there by herself, he approached her with all possible respect and courtesy. Noticing, after having paid the usual compliments, that she looked very sad, he said:

'I do not understand, Madam, how a person as beautiful as you are can be sad as you appear to be; for, although I may pride myself on having seen a vast number of beautiful ladies, I can truthfully say that I have never seen one whose beauty approaches yours.'

'You are pleased to say so, sir,' replied the Princess, and stopped there.

'Beauty,' Rickey with the Tuft went on, 'is such a great asset that it must surely replace everything else and, when one possesses it, I do not see how anything could afflict one very much.'

'I would rather,' said the Princess, 'be as ugly as you and have some wits, than have beauty like mine and be as stupid as I am.'

'Nothing, Madam, proves more clearly that one has intelligence than to believe that one has none. It is in the nature of this quality that, the more one has of it, the more one feels the lack of it.'

'I didn't know that,' said the Princess. 'But I do know that I am very stupid, and that is why I am so miserable.'

'If that is all, Madam, I can easily relieve your distress.'

'And how will you manage that?' asked the Princess.

'I have the power,' said Rickey with the Tuft, 'to give as much wit as anyone could have to the person whom I love most, and since you, Madam, are that person, it depends only on you to have as much wit as anyone can have by saying that you are willing to marry me.'

The Princess was quite dumbfounded and made no answer.

'I see,' Rickey with the Tuft went on, 'that you find this a hard offer to accept, and I am not surprised; but I give you a whole year to make up your mind to it.'

The Princess had so little wit, and at the same time so longed to have some, that she imagined that the end of the year would never come and accepted the offer which was made to her.

No sooner had she promised Rickey with the Tuft that she would marry him in a year's time to the day, than she felt herself becoming quite different. She found that she had no difficulty at all in saying whatever came into her head, and that she could say it in a witty, agreeable and natural way. She at once began a long, bantering conversation with Rickey with the Tuft, in which she shone so much that Rickey wondered whether he had not given her more wit than he had kept for himself.

When she returned to the palace, no one knew what to make of this sudden and extraordinary change, for now she was as sensible and as witty as she had been foolish before. The whole Court were in raptures. Only her younger sister was not pleased, because, having no longer the advantage of intelligence over her, she appeared beside her as a most unattractive frump.

The King let himself be guided by her advice, and sometimes even held his council in her apartments. The rumour of the change spread quickly and all the young princes of the neighbouring kingdoms competed to win her favour, almost all of them asking her hand in marriage. But she found none who had wit enough for her and she listened to them all without accepting any.

However, one came who was so powerful, so rich, so intelligent and so handsome that she could not help conceiving a liking for him. Her father noticed this and told her that the choice of a husband lay in her own hands and that she had only to declare her preference. But the more intelligent one is, the harder it is to reach a definite decision on this particular matter, so she thanked her father and asked for time to think it over.

In order to reflect quietly on what she ought to do, she went, as it happened, for a walk in the same wood in which she had met Rickey with the Tuft. She was walking along, deep in thought, when she heard a muffled noise coming from under her feet, as though a number of people were hurrying busily to and fro. Listening more carefully, she heard someone say: 'Bring me that stewpot,' someone else: 'Hand me that cauldron,' and another: 'Put some wood on the fire.' At the same moment the ground opened and she saw at her feet what appeared to be a huge kitchen full of cooks, kitchen-boys, and all the servants necessary to prepare a great banquet. A column of twenty or thirty roasting-cooks came marching out and took up their position round a very long table in a glade of the wood and then, with their larding-pins in their hands and their fox-fur bonnets on their heads, began to work in unison, to the chant of a rhythmic song.

Astonished at this sight, the Princess asked them for whom they were working.

'Why, Madam,' said the one who appeared to be

the leader, 'for Prince Rickey with the Tuft. His wedding is to-morrow.'

The Princess, more surprised than ever, and suddenly remembering that it was a year to the day since she had promised to marry Prince Rickey with the Tuft, almost jumped out of her skin. The reason why she had not remembered before was that, when she made her promise, she was still very foolish; and, when she had the new wits which the Prince had given her, all her foolish thoughts were forgotten.

She had not gone many steps further, continuing her walk, when Rickey with the Tuft appeared before her, most richly and elegantly dressed, like a prince on the way to his wedding.

'You see me, Madam,' he said, 'punctually keeping my promise. I do not doubt that you are here to keep yours and to make me the happiest of men by giving me your hand.'

'I must tell you frankly,' the Princess replied, 'that I have not yet made my mind up on the question, and I do not think I can ever make it up in the way that you wish.'

'You amaze me,' said Rickey with the Tuft.

'I expect so,' said the Princess. 'And naturally, if I were dealing with some churlish fellow, with a man of no intelligence, I should feel highly embarrassed. "The word of a princess is binding," he would say, "and you must marry me because you have promised to." But as the man to whom I am speaking is the most intelligent man in the world, I am sure that he will listen to reason. You know that, when I was still very foolish, I could not make up my mind to marry you. Can you expect that, with the wit you have given me, which makes me even more fastidious about people than I was, I should take a decision to-day which I could not take at that time? If you seriously meant to marry me, you made a great mistake in taking away my stupidity and causing me to see more clearly now than I did then.'

'If, as you have just said,' replied Rickey with the Tuft, 'you would think a stupid man justified in reproaching you for breaking your promise, can you expect that I should not do the same, Madam, since the whole of my life's happiness is at stake? Is it reasonable to suppose that people who possess intelligence should be content with less than those who have none? Can you maintain that, you who have so much and who so longed to have it? But, with your permission, let us come to the point. Apart from my ugliness, is there anything in me which displeases you? Are you dissatisfied with my breeding, my wit, my character, or my manner?'

'By no means,' said the Princess. 'I like in you all the things that you have just said.'

'If that is the case,' rejoined Rickey with the Tuft, 'I am going to be happy, since you can make me the most desirable of men.'

'How can that be?' asked the Princess.

'That can be,' Rickey with the Tuft replied, 'if you like me well enough to wish that it should be. And to put an end to your hesitation, let me tell you that the same fairy who, on my birthday, gave me the power of bestowing intelligence on the person I was to like best, also gave you the power of bestowing good looks on the person you were to love, provided you were willing to do him that favour.'

'If that is the case,' said the Princess, 'I wish with all my heart that you should become the most handsome and the most desirable of princes. I make you that gift, so far as it lies in me.'

No sooner had the Princess uttered these words than Rickey with the Tuft became in her eyes the most handsome, the most attractive, and the most desirable man she had ever seen.

Some people maintain that the change was brought about, not by the fairy's spells, but by love alone. They say that the Princess, having considered her lover's perseverance, his tact, and all his qualities of mind and spirit, no longer saw his deformities or the ugliness of his face; that his hump appeared only as a graceful stoop and that, whereas until then he had seemed to walk with a dreadful limp, she now saw only a slight sway which fascinated her. They also say that his eyes, which crossed, seemed to her to shine all the brighter for that; that what she had taken for a squint now struck her merely as a sign of intense passion, and that even his large red nose had for her something martial and heroic about it.

Whatever the truth may be, the Princess promised on the spot that she would marry him, provided that he obtained the consent of the King her father. The King, learning that his daughter thought so highly of Rickey with the Tuft, of whom he had heard from other sources as a most wise and intelligent prince, welcomed him as his son-in-law. The wedding took place on the next day, exactly as Rickey with the Tuft had foreseen, and according to the orders which he had given many months before.

MORAL

All that you find written here
Is less a tale than solemn truth.
Handsome is what we hold dear,
Those we love are not uncouth.

SECOND MORAL

A person to whom nature
Had given beauty of feature,
A skin outmatching art
In perfect loveliness,
With all such gifts would less
Have power to touch the heart
Than one in whom love suddenly revealed
A single grace to other eyes concealed.